Passwords and Security

Eric Minton

PowerKiDS press
New York

Published in 2014 by The Rosen Publishing Group, Inc.
29 East 21st Street, New York, NY 10010

Copyright © 2014 by The Rosen Publishing Group, Inc.

All rights reserved. No part of this book may be reproduced in any form without permission in writing from the publisher, except by a reviewer.

First Edition

Editor: Amelie von Zumbusch
Photo Research: Katie Stryker
Book Design: Colleen Bialecki
Book Layout: Joe Carney

Photo Credits: Cover Jupiterimages/Brand X Pictures/Getty Images; p. 5 Blend Images/Thinkstock; p. 6 Jupiterimages/Stockbyte/Thinkstock; p. 7 Peter Fuchs/Shutterstock.com; pp. 8, 29 iStock/Thinkstock; p. 9 Image Source/Getty Images; pp. 10, 14, 27 Fuse/Thinkstock; p. 11 racorn/Shutterstock.com; p. 13 Jack Hollingsworth/Photodisc/Thinkstock; p. 15 CroMary/Shutterstock.com; p. 17 Jose Luis Pelaez Inc/Blend Images/Getty Images; p. 18 Ciaran Griffin/Stockbyte/Thinkstock; p. 19 Palomino Productions/Brand X Pictures/Getty Images; p. 20 Hemera/Thinkstock; p. 21 Jupiterimages/Pixland/Thinkstock; p. 23 Imagesbybarbara/E+/Getty Images; p. 24 Justin Sullivan/Getty Images; p. 25 315 studio/Shutterstock.com; p. 28 Hero Images/Getty Images.

Library of Congress Cataloging-in-Publication Data

Minton, Eric.
 Passwords and security / by Eric Minton. — 1st edition.
    pages cm. — (Stay safe online)
 Includes index.
 ISBN 978-1-4777-2942-7 (library binding) — ISBN 978-1-4777-3024-9 (pbk.) —
 ISBN 978-1-4777-3095-9 (6-pack)
 1. Internet—Safety measures—Juvenile literature. 2. Computer security—Juvenile literature.
 3. Internet and children—Juvenile literature. I. Title.
 TK5105.875.I57M5577 2014
 005.8—dc23
                                        2013033101

Manufactured in the United States of America

CPSIA Compliance Information: Batch # W14PK2: For Further Information contact Rosen Publishing, New York, New York at 1-800-237-9932

Contents

Online Security 4
The Importance of Privacy 6
Choosing Passwords 8
Password Security 10
Other Security Tools 14
Phishing and Hacking 16
If You've Been Hacked 20
Outside the House 22
Browser Cookies 24
Protecting Your Information 26
Be Smart and Safe 30
Glossary 31
Index 32
Websites 32

Online Security

Online security protects your online **accounts** from Internet criminals. It keeps your accounts safe in the same way that door locks and burglar alarms keep criminals out of your home.

Without online security, anyone could log into your accounts. Someone could steal your character in an online game, read your private emails, or make embarrassing posts under your name on your **social media** accounts.

A password is a series of **characters** that works like the combination lock on a school locker. Only someone who knows the password can get into the account it protects. Each of your online accounts needs a password. This includes email accounts, social media sites, message boards, and online video games. Home computers, **Wi-Fi** networks, and smartphones need passwords, too.

> Your passwords keep your online accounts safe. They also protect the devices, such as smartphones and computers, that you use to access those accounts.

The Importance of Privacy

Other people can learn a lot about you online. Anyone who visits a forum or is friends with you on a social media website can read everything that you post there.

Your emails, photos, instant messages, and text messages can be copied and forwarded to countless people. They can even be posted publicly for everyone to see.

> A diary with a lock on it is a private place to write down your thoughts. A comment on a public forum or blog is not.

It takes just seconds for someone to forward an email or text that you sent him to somebody else.

You never know who's reading your posts and messages. It might not just be friends and family. Bullies and complete strangers might be able to see them, too.

Someone can use this information to hurt you. For example, a silly photograph or video that was fun to send to a friend would be really embarrassing if a bully posted it for all of your classmates to see.

Choosing Passwords

When you make up a password, choose one that's hard to guess. Never use a password that's easy for someone who knows you to figure out. This includes passwords based on your first or last name, birthday, street address, phone number, or favorite teams or musical group.

Never include your birthday as part of your password. That makes for a password that is far too easy to guess.

Every character you add to your password makes it much harder for a hacker to guess.

Hackers can use computer programs to guess your password. These allow a hacker to find out any password that is short and simple. Many of these programs use dictionaries that can guess any password that is made from real words.

A good password should be at least 14 characters long, but longer is better. Your password should also use a wide range of characters. Include uppercase letters, lowercase letters, numbers, and symbols such as question marks and exclamation points.

Did You Know?

The first letter of each word in a sentence can make a memorable and secure password. "I bought my first Superman comic book at Ron's Comic Shop for three dollars" becomes "IbmfScb@RCS43$."

Password Security

Your password needs to be secret to do its job. Anyone who learns your password can log in under your name and read your messages. He can also send messages using your name. It's best not to share your password with anyone.

If you must share your password, do it privately. Someone may read it if you write it down or send it by email. Someone may overhear if you speak it in a public place or over the phone.

Don't tell your password to anyone, even your best friend!

When you are typing in your password, make sure that nobody can see what you are typing.

The safest place to store your password is in your head. If you need to write it down, put it in a safe place where no one else will find it. Make it look like something other than a password. Don't keep it near your computer.

Did You Know?

Password-management programs such as LastPass and KeePass keep track of all your passwords. They create complicated, hard-to-guess passwords and remember them for you.

Pick a different password for each of your accounts. If you use the same password for your email and your favorite social media account, someone who gets into one can use the same password to get into the other.

Changing your passwords regularly throws off anyone who has learned your password and wants to use it to spy on you. Change passwords every three months or whenever you log in from a public computer or Wi-Fi **hotspot**.

Be careful with sharing your passwords. A friend might decide to play a prank using your password. He might also use it to get revenge if he gets angry with you. Be ready to change any password that you've shared.

> Don't reuse old passwords. If you do, anyone who learned your old password could use it to get into your account.

Other Security Tools

Passwords aren't the only tools that help keep your information secure online. Some websites show you a picture, such as a cat or a flower, and ask you to type the name of what's in the picture. This keeps out the password-guessing programs that hackers and **spammers** use.

A CAPTCHA is a piece of twisted, multicolored text that is hard for computer programs to read. Some websites ask you to read a CAPTCHA and type the characters in it into a box.

The most secure answers to security questions are false answers because they're hard to guess.

To unlock some Android smartphones, you draw a pattern on the phone's screen. This is often called a screen lock pattern.

A security question is a question that you know the answer to but strangers wouldn't, such as your first pet's name. If you forget your password, you can pick a new one after answering your security question.

Did You Know?

Biometric security looks at unique things about you like your fingerprints or voice. These are good for security because they're hard to fake. A few computers and smartphones use biometrics.

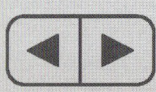

Phishing and Hacking

Some hackers try to trick you with emails that look like they're from the website of a well-known company. The fake emails ask you for your password or other personal information. This trickery is called **phishing**.

Phishing emails use links that look like they go to a real website or email address. They actually go to a fake site or email address that the hacker controls. There, you're asked to type your password or give your credit card number. The hacker can use this information to steal from you.

Phishing doesn't just happen online. Some hackers phish for passwords by phone. Never give out personal information to a stranger over the phone.

> Some phishing emails are very convincing. They look official and use real logos copied from company websites.

Hackers can steal your password even when you're not online. They use computer programs that can guess billions of different passwords every second. The more complicated your password is, the harder it is for these programs to guess. The most important element in making a secure password is length. Longer is always better, as long as it's not too long to remember.

Over the years, hackers have gotten better at figuring out passwords. One trick that people used to use to create passwords was to replace characters in a word with numbers or symbols, such as replacing "a" with @.

It's very important to have a strong password. After all, that is the main way to keep your online accounts safe from hackers.

Try making up a password based on a sentence. For example, "M<3aaGr8Daep" is based on the sentence "My favorite animals are Great Danes and emperor penguins."

Turning "password" into "p@55w0rd" is one example of this. Another was capitalizing the first letter of a word or adding punctuation at the end. Password experts no longer recommend these tricks since hackers use programs that look for them.

Did You Know?

Keyloggers are computer **viruses** that read everything you type, including your password. They're most common on public computers, like those in libraries or Internet cafés.

19

If You've Been Hacked

If you think someone has learned your password or hacked your account, change your password right away. Signs of hacking include new posts or emails that you didn't write and strange links in your profile or signature file.

If your password doesn't get you into your account, reset the password using your security questions. This won't work if the hacker changed your security questions. You'll have to call or email the website's owners for help.

If you think that your account has been hacked, tell your parent or guardian immediately.

If your account was hacked, you might need to get a parent or other adult to contact the company that the account was with.

A hacker who knows your password can break into every account protected with that password. If you used that password for other accounts, change your password on them, too. Change your security questions along with your passwords. Of course, it's best never to use passwords for more than one account.

Outside the House

Always log out properly from any online account you use on a public computer. Closing a browser tab or window doesn't log you out. Neither does quitting out of the web browser. If you don't log out, anyone can walk up to the computer and use your account.

Some websites have boxes that you can click that tell the site to fill in your user name and password automatically when you visit the site from a particular computer. Never use this feature on a public computer.

Watch out for shoulder surfing. This is when someone looks over your shoulder to see what you're typing on a computer or smartphone. Make sure no one is close enough to read your password or other private information.

The computers in schools and libraries are public computers.

Did You Know?

Public computers are more likely to be infected with computer viruses. Always check your files for viruses if you use a public computer to work on them.

 Browser Cookies

Websites store information on your web browser in files called **cookies**. Cookies can remember things like screen names and passwords, when you last visited a site, or what you've bought online. Websites use this information to recommend things for you to buy and to pick advertisements to show you.

> Be aware of apps, including map and weather apps, that ask for your location. When you are done using those apps, turn the location feature off.

The cookies in your web browser are likely behind your getting ads for dog food and dog toys after you have done a web search for dog care.

If a hacker gets into your computer, she can read your cookies to steal personal information. You can go into your browser's preferences to delete some or all cookies, block new cookies, and allow or block cookies from specific websites.

Some smartphone apps, such as certain games, can look at your location, your **contact list**, and your photos. If you can, turn this feature of the app off. If you can't, delete the app.

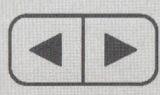

Protecting Your Information

A **privacy policy** is an explanation of what a website's owners will do with any personal information that you type in. This includes your name, age, email address, home address, and credit card numbers. Depending on the policy, this can mean that the website's owners can share your personal information with other people. It can also mean that they own any stories, music, photos, or videos that you make and post on their site.

Privacy policies are written using legal language, which is hard for anyone who is not a lawyer to understand. Have a trusted adult help you understand what is in each website's privacy policy. The adult can advise you on whether or not to agree to the policy.

> Privacy policies can be very confusing. You should always talk to an adult before agreeing to one.

Antivirus software will help keep your tablet, smartphone, or computer running smoothly.

This flash drive is being plugged into a laptop computer. Flash drives are small, light, and easy to carry around.

A hacker who breaks into your online accounts can delete your files or give your computer a virus. You need to plan ahead to protect yourself. Once something bad happens, it may be too late to fix it.

Antivirus software helps protect your computer against viruses. Talk to your parents about installing an antivirus program on your computer. Always listen to your antivirus software's warnings. Never visit a website or open a file that your antivirus software says may be dangerous.

Back up important files and store them somewhere other than your computer. You might use a **flash drive** or **file-hosting service** like Dropbox. You need to keep your files safe even if your computer is attacked by a virus, broken, or stolen.

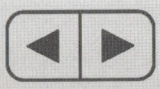

Be Smart and Safe

1. Some websites or computers limit your password to a maximum length, such as 8 or 16 characters. Make your password as long as possible.

2. Obvious passwords like "password" or "12345678" are so easy to guess that anyone can figure them out. Don't use them.

3. Using a real word or name as a password is especially unsafe. Hackers often use "dictionary attack" programs to guess every word in the dictionary quickly.

4. Using letters from a long phrase makes for a secure password, as long as it is not a well-known phrase.

5. To get into Android smartphones, you can draw a pattern instead of entering a password. Pick a complicated, unusual pattern. Wipe your fingermarks off the screen afterwards.

6. Changing passwords too often can do more harm than good if you can't remember your new passwords.

7. If you learn that a website you visit has been attacked by a hacker, change your password on that site immediately.

Glossary

accounts (uh-KOWNTS) Things that a business supplies to people who regularly use its services.

characters (KER-ik-turz) Symbols used in writing, such as letters or numbers.

contact list (KON-takt LIST) A group of email addresses or screen names.

cookies (KU-keez) Things attached to web browsers that gather information about web users.

file-hosting service (FYL-hohst-ing SER-vis) A company or other group that provides room for people to store files online.

flash drive (FLASH DRYV) A small thing used to store computer files.

hackers (HA-kerz) People who break into email accounts or other computer systems.

hotspot (HOT-spot) An area in which there is free Internet access.

phishing (FIH-shing) Posing as a real company to trick people into sharing personal information.

privacy policy (PRY-vuh-see PAH-luh-see) The agreement that lays out how a website can use personal information from its users.

social media (SOH-shul MEE-dee-uh) Having to do with online communities through which people share information, messages, photos, videos, and thoughts.

spammers (SPAM-erz) People who send unwanted email messages.

viruses (VY-rus-ez) Programs that harm a computer.

Wi-Fi (WY-FY) Using radio waves to connect to the Internet.

Index

A
account(s), 4, 12, 20–22, 29

C
characters, 4, 9, 14, 18, 30
computer(s), 4, 11–12, 15, 19, 22, 25, 29–30

E
email(s), 4, 6, 10, 12, 16, 20

F
file-hosting service, 29

G
game(s), 4, 25

H
hacker(s), 9, 14, 16, 18–21, 25, 29, 30
hotspot, 12

I
information, 7, 14, 16, 22, 24–26

M
message boards, 4
messages, 6–7, 10

N
networks, 4

P
photo(s), 6–7, 25–26
posts, 4, 7, 20
privacy policy, 26

S
series, 4
smartphone(s), 4, 22, 30
social media sites, 4
spammers, 14
stranger(s), 7, 15–16

V
video(s), 7, 26
virus(es), 29

Websites

Due to the changing nature of Internet links, PowerKids Press has developed an online list of websites related to the subject of this book. This site is updated regularly. Please use this link to access the list: www.powerkidslinks.com/sso/secure/